KABUNGO

KABUNGO

ROLLI

Illustrations by
Milan Pavlovic

Groundwood Books
House of Anansi Press
Toronto   Berkeley

Text copyright © 2016 by Rolli
Published in Canada and the USA in 2016 by Groundwood Books

A few extracts from *Kabungo* were first published in *knowonder!* magazine and two of
their anthologies — *The White Sail* and *Nerissa's Celebration*.

Groundwood Books / House of Anansi Press
groundwoodbooks.com

We acknowledge for their financial support of our publishing program the Canada
Council for the Arts, the Ontario Arts Council and the Government of Canada.

With the participation of the Government of Canada
Avec la participation du gouvernement du Canada | Canadä

Library and Archives Canada Cataloguing in Publication
Rolli, author
Kabungo / Rolli ; illustrated by Milan Pavlovic.
Issued in print and electronic formats.
ISBN 978-1-55498-804-4 (bound). — ISBN 978-1-55498-806-8 (html).
— ISBN 978-1-55498-812-9 (mobi)
I. Pavlovic, Milan, illustrator II. Title.
PS8635.O4465K33 2016   jC813'.6   C2015-903588-0
C2015-903589-9

Groundwood Books is committed to protecting our natural environment. As part of our
efforts, the interior of this book is printed on paper that contains 100% post-consumer
recycled fibers, is acid-free and is processed chlorine-free.

Illustrations by Milan Pavlovic
Design by Michael Solomon
Printed and bound in Canada

MIX
Paper from
responsible sources
FSC® C016245

For Olga

Contents

ONE
Shark Toofs

MY FRIEND KABUNGO lives in a cave on Main Street. It's right by the post office.

One day, I banged on the side of the cave with a rock. Caves don't have doors, unfortunately.

A pair of eyes sparkled in the dark.

"Which?" said a deep voice. Kabungo has a surprisingly deep voice for a ten-year-old girl.

"It's just me," I said. "Beverly."

"Ohhh kay," said my friend, waving her hand. "In."

Even after I took off my sunglasses, it was still black in the cave.

Kabungo is used to it. She can see in the dark like a tiger.

I asked her to switch the lights on.

Kabungo knew what I meant. There was a crumpling sound, then a thump and then — presto — a flame appeared in the fire pit.

Kabungo doesn't have electricity. She doesn't have a lot of things. She has a table, though I don't think she uses it. She has some cutlery I brought her (I *know* she doesn't use that). She has a black-and-white TV. I guess it's for decoration.

"How Belly?" she said. Kabungo has always called me Belly. I don't think she has enough teeth to say Beverly.

"Fine, K," I said. Sometimes I call her K for short. "How about you?"

"Mmm." She scratched her head. "Itchy."

"Have you been using your flea powder?" I bought her some a while back.

"Nnnn," said Kabungo, shaking her head. "Not tasty."

I would have told her that flea powder wasn't for eating, but I never tell anyone anything more than a hundred times. It's my personal rule.

As usual, there were cobwebs in every corner and dust bunnies running wild. I don't care for dust or spiders, but Kabungo doesn't seem to mind.

There was something different about the cave that day. I couldn't quite put my finger on it — until I put my hand on it. I leaned on the table and felt something sharp.

It was a string with a bunch of pointy white things threaded onto it. A little hammer lay next to it, too, and a nail.

"What are you making?" I asked.

"Juleree." Kabungo pointed to my bead necklace. "Like Belly."

I took a closer look at the white things. They looked like ... teeth.

"K? What are these?"

"Shark toofs," she whispered seriously. "Shhh. Secret toofs."

"You mean *teeth*," I said. *Without grammar, words are worthless.* My English teacher, Ms. Beaux-Beaux, is always saying that.

"Ya, ya. Teefs."

I gave up.

"So where did you get them?" I asked, holding one up to the fire.

"Jo's Ocean," she said even more seriously. "Shh."

I had zero idea what she meant. Star City, where we live, is nowhere near the ocean.

14

And I didn't know anyone named Jo.

"I cotch toofs, shh. In Jo's Ocean. Belly help cotch?"

I was about to say, "No way," but then I thought it might be a good idea to find out where she was getting these teeth. I consider it my personal mission to keep Kabungo out of prison.

So I told her, "Okay. Let's go."

As I turned away, Kabungo grabbed my sleeve.

"Nnn," she said. "Wait. Sungo."

Sungo means night to Kabungo. And sunup means day. I've tried teaching her the proper terms, but she just doesn't remember. So I told her I'd be back at sungo.

"Promise, Belly?" she said, looking worried. Kabungo has trouble trusting people.

"Promise," I said.

Kabungo smiled. As I waved goodbye, I reminded myself to buy her another toothbrush.

◉

The sun sets pretty late in Star City. It was nine o'clock when I reached the cave.

"Ready, Belly," said Kabungo, stepping out of the shadows.

She sure *was* ready. She had on her "beast furs" — made from what animal, I have no idea — and her snakeskin pouch. There were smudges of red paint on her forehead and under her eyes.

"Belly come!" she said. "Sniff Kabungo."

To Kabungo sniff just means follow. Maybe because dogs follow a scent by sniffing? That's just a guess.

I sniffed Kabungo across Main Street,

through Mr. Banbury's backyard and down the alley. It was dark in the alley. About all I could see was the snakeskin pouch sparkling in the starlight. All I could hear was the crunching of leaves underfoot. So I followed the sparkle and the leaf-crunch and just tried my hardest not to run into any of the trees that lined the alley.

It's a good thing Kabungo has tiger eyes.

Finally, she pushed through some branches and ...

"Here," said Kabungo.

She pointed at a long orange building with a yellow sign. The Sunset Club.

The Sunset Club isn't really a club. It's a retirement home for older people. My Uncle George has an apartment there. It smells like peppermints.

"*This* is Jo's Ocean?" I said.

Kabungo shook her head.

"*In*," she said. "Sniff. Shh."

I sniffed her around the building to the fifth window on the ground floor. It was a surprisingly warm night for October, so most of the windows were wide open.

"In," she said again softly. "Shh. *Shh*. Ocean."

"K!" I whispered. "You can't go in there."

But it was too late. She sprang through the window like a wildcat. I leaned through it trying to pull her back, when she reached out, pulled me in and plopped me on the floor.

For a ten-year-old, Kabungo is mighty.

"Kabungo!" I hissed. "We're breaking the law!"

But she just shook her head and said, "No breaks, Belly. Carful. Shh." And she tiptoed across the room.

I squinted. It was dark, but I could still make out a few things. I could see ... a fish tank. A pair of armchairs. A bookcase full of books.

Hmm, I thought, as I weaved my way through the furniture. *There's something*

familiar about all this. I was too nervous, though, to figure out what. I don't like breaking the law.

I followed Kabungo into a kitchen, down a hall and into a dark room. She was moving really slowly now, almost like she was hunting.

I moved even slower. Because it was so dark, I could hardly see.

I bumped into something. Something soft. I was pretty sure it was a bed. I waited for my eyes to adjust.

It *was* a bed.

My ears twitched. I could hear snoring.

Someone was *in* the bed.

My nose twitched. I sniffed the air. It smelled like …

Peppermints.

Now I knew whose apartment it was, and who lay snoozing in the bed. I wondered what

on earth Kabungo could want in my Uncle George's apartment.

And then I didn't have to wonder, because I could see ...

Okay, lots of older people run out of teeth. It's no big deal. They just go out and buy new ones, false ones. I didn't realize my Uncle George had false teeth but he must have, because there was a nice shiny pair sitting in a glass of water on his nightstand.

As my Uncle George snored, Kabungo slowly reached into the glass of water and ... *snatched his teeth!* Snatched them and stuffed them into her snakeskin pouch.

It was all over and done before I had time to say or do anything. And the second the teeth were in her pouch, Kabungo skipped out of the bedroom, down the hall and back out the window.

For a while I stood there wondering what to do, what the *proper course of action* might be. I considered waking my uncle, but I just wasn't sure how to tell him that his false teeth had been stolen in the night by a cavegirl.

It really was a unique scenario. Most scenarios involving Kabungo are.

In the end, I decided to track down Kabungo before she could get into any more trouble.

By the time I squeezed back out the window, there was no sign of her.

"Oh, Kabungo," I said to myself.

I peeked through a few windows and didn't see anything, so I decided just to head to the cave. Only this time, I skipped the back alleys and stuck to the streets. It took a bit longer, but at least I could tell where I was going.

People say exercise is great for your brain.

It's true. It wasn't until I was racing back to the cave that it hit me.

Jo's Ocean.

"Jo" was probably as close to "George" as Kabungo could manage with her cave-teeth. And the "ocean" had to be my uncle's water glass.

Jo's Ocean. Shark toofs.

There was a light flickering in the cave, so I let myself in and … gasped. Because Kabungo was *dancing*. I mean, if you could call it dancing. I'd really never seen anything like it. She was hopping around on one foot and swinging her arms and scratching herself.

It reminded me of gymnastics or running from bees. It was astonishing.

As soon as she noticed me, she smiled.

"Itchy dance," she explained, still moving.

23

I raised my eyebrows and wondered if she meant victory dance.

There was always a chance that she was just itchy. She does have fleas.

"K," I said. "We need to talk."

"Mmm? Oh kay."

Kabungo sat down on the floor. I looked for the least dirty spot and sat down, too.

"Do you remember what I told you, K, about going into other people's houses?"

"Ya," said Kabungo, scratching her elbow.

"And you remember what I told you about taking stuff that's not yours?"

"Ya, ya." She scratched her knee.

"Okay. Then why on earth did —"

"Look, Belly!" cried my friend. She jumped up and ran over to the table. She pointed at something.

I got up. I walked over to the table. I looked down ...

There they were. My Uncle George's false teeth. They were sitting next to the hammer and the necklace. Luckily they were still in one piece, because my uncle would have found it pretty hard to chew his food with a necklace.

"See?" said Kabungo. "Toofs. Juleree, Belly. See?"

She picked up the little hammer lying next to the teeth, swung it back and —

"Kabungo, stop!" I cried.

She stopped. Thank goodness. And set down the hammer.

"Belly, what?" she said, looking surprised. "Not juleree?"

I wasn't sure what to say, because I had too *much* to say. When there are too many of

them, words can plug up your brain.

"You," she went on. "Juleree present, Bel-ly. Toofs. *You*." She picked up the necklace and slipped it over my head. She stood there smiling at me.

In the end, there was only one thing I could say ...

"Oh, Kabungo."

TWO
Targur

FOR A LONG TIME, my major goal in life was to teach Kabungo the alphabet. It just seemed like a shame that a ten-year-old girl who lived in a cave on Main Street couldn't read or write or even sign her name.

If teaching a cavegirl her ABCs sounds hard, though, think harder. Think impossible. Because it's practically impossible to teach someone something when she keeps eating bugs and smelling your hair.

But I kept trying. As my Uncle George always says, sooner or later, even impossible

takes a nap.

So I headed to the cave one day with a few books under my arm. They were all picture books. Kabungo doesn't have the patience for too many words. I tried reading her a novel once but she just said, "Yak, yak, yak," and threw it into the fire pit.

We started out that day with *Amazing A to Z*, an alphabet book.

It didn't go very well. Kabungo tried to bite the apple in "A for Apple." I wasn't looking forward to explaining the teeth marks to Ms. Keating, the librarian.

When we got to "E for Elephant," she hid under the table and wouldn't come out until I promised her that elephants weren't real.

That counts as a lie, I know. But when it comes to teaching a cavegirl, lying is sometimes necessary.

After my friend tried crumpling the "S for Snake" page, I decided to call it a day.

I was just about to shut the book when Kabungo stopped me.

"What?" she said, pointing at the next page.

"That," I said, "is a tiger. *T* for *Tiger*."

"Mmm," said my friend, chewing her finger. When Kabungo is thinking, she always looks straight up and chews her finger. "Want that," she said finally, nodding hard.

"You want a tiger, K?"

She nodded even harder.

"Ya. Soft. Targur soft nice, Belly."

I carefully explained that tigers are large and dangerous and only live in jungles and zoos. But I could tell she wasn't listening.

When Kabungo isn't listening, she gets these *bubble* eyes. I just know there's a

thought bubble over her head with a tiger in it or a pork chop or whatever she's thinking about at the time.

She just kept staring at the picture of the tiger and trying to rub its fur. So I told her that, if she wanted, I could bring her a whole book about tigers.

That got her attention.

"Ya, ya, Belly," she said. "Fetch me. Go."

So I gathered up the books (but not the alphabet book, which she wouldn't give back) and headed out.

I was just stepping into the sunlight when a voice behind me said, "Oh, Belly?"

"Yes, K?"

"Bring targur, too."

And before I could answer, she ducked back into the shadows.

◉

Finding a tiger for a cavegirl was really not how I'd planned on spending my afternoon.

Luckily, I had an idea ...

If you took a candy store and a medicine store and about a dozen other stores and rubbed them together, what you'd probably end up with is Gobshaw's Drug Shop. It's right across from the library.

Mr. Gobshaw is a great guy. Even though he has no hair, he never quits smiling. His favorite expression is "Welcome! We have everything!"

And it's true.

So when I walked into his store and asked him if he had any tigers, it's not like I thought he wouldn't. I just wanted to know where to look.

"Of course we have tigers!" he cried. "They're next to the breath mints."

I checked out the tigers (stuffed, of course) and picked the one that looked the strongest. Kabungo can be a little rough with her things.

"Circus is in town," said Mr. Gobshaw as he handed me my change.

"Is it?" I said.

"Yup." He stuffed the tiger into a bag. "Mossgrove's Orange Circus. All week. How about a couple of tickets?"

"No, thanks," I said. I've never really liked circuses too much. They're crowded. Also, they smell bad.

"You sure? I can give 'em to you for half price."

"How much are they?" I asked. Not that I really wanted any.

"They're free," said Mr. Gobshaw. "For kids, they're always free."

"It's a good deal! I'd take it!" said Mrs.

Gobshaw, popping her head out of the back room, then popping it right back in again.

Mr. Gobshaw crossed his arms.

"You drive a hard bargain," he said. "I'll tell you what. You can have 'em ... for 75 percent off."

"Off free?" I said.

"Yup," said Mr. Gobshaw. "And that's my final offer."

"Nah," I said. "But thanks anyway."

"Sold!" cried Mr. Gobshaw. He stuck two tickets into my bag and handed it to me. "Thanks for shopping at Gobshaw's Drug Shop. Remember — we have everything!"

As I walked out of the store, I looked back. Mr. Gobshaw had a big smile on his face.

He has a pretty strange sense of humor. I've always liked that about him.

Next I crossed the street to the Star City

Public Library and picked out a picture book called *Twylla and the Tiger*. Ms. Keating raised her eyebrows (I hadn't read that book since I was four) but didn't ask any questions.

I stuck the book into the bag with the stuffed animal and made my way back to the cave.

The fire was burning bright. But there was no sign of Kabungo.

"K?" I said, looking around. "K?"

"Go way!" said a scared voice.

"K? Is that you? Where are you?"

"Go way . . . elphant!" The voice was coming from under the table.

I crouched down. Kabungo was sitting on the floor with her knees drawn up to her chest, shivering.

"Oh, Belly!" she cried.

"Oh, Kabungo," I sighed. Halloween was

coming up soon. If she was spooked by a cartoon elephant, I wondered how she'd react to vampires.

It took a while, but I got her to come out from under the table. Then I pulled out *Twylla and the Tiger*.

"Ya, ya!" said Kabungo right away. "Bring targur too, Belly?"

I told her I did bring her a tiger. But first we had to read the book.

Kabungo chewed her finger.

"Oh kay," she said at last. "Go, go!"

As I read the book, an amazing thing happened. Kabungo actually sat still. She paid attention. She listened. She was so excited to get to the next page and the next that she sometimes flipped the page for me.

I was impressed.

"Now targur, Belly?" my friend said as

I put the book away. "Targur, right? Member?"

I took a deep breath, pulled the tiger out of the bag and passed it to her.

As Kabungo examined the tiger, I watched her face carefully. She didn't make her sweet

face, which means she likes something. She didn't make her lemon face, either.

She really didn't make any face at all. She just flipped the tiger over a few times, sniffed it once and — threw it into the fire.

"Kabungo!" I cried. "That cost $6.99!"

"Nope," she said, crossing her arms. "Not. Targur. *Real* targur, Belly. Better try. Go."

And before I could say "but" my friend took me by the arm, walked me out of the cave and waved goodbye.

I took the long way home that night. So I could think.

I was 93 percent sure Kabungo didn't understand what a tiger was, how big it was, how dangerous . . .

That was it. I was so sure I had a lightbulb over my head, I almost reached up and checked.

But instead I reached down into my bag

and pulled out the pair of tickets to Moss-grove's Orange Circus.

◉

Thinking back, probably the biggest mis-take of my life was taking Kabungo to the cir-cus. Even remembering it gives me a headache.

When Kabungo saw a girl in a feathery costume, she shouted, "Turkey bird!" and chased her up and down the aisles until the security guard said, "This is your first warn-ing, kid."

When Kabungo saw The Astonishing Mossgrove walk out with his Acrobatic El-ephant, she hid under her chair and kicked and screamed until the elephant ran back into its cage and the security guard said, "This is your *second* warning, kid."

When Kabungo finally saw Louis — that

was the tiger's name — she looked at me angrily and said, "Nope. Not. Targur. Too big. Targur small nice, Belly. Soft. Better try." Then she stood on her chair and booed until the security guard looked at her like he was about to say, "This is your third and final warning, kid."

But he didn't have to. Because Kabungo grabbed me by the hand and practically dragged me back to the cave.

I took the extra-long way back home that day. Sometimes I get so mad at Kabungo, I want to move to Cincinnati. But then I think of how helpless she'd be without me, in her big lonesome cave, without any flea powder.

When you don't know what to do, it pays to look at a bulletin board. They help take your mind off things and they're full of useful information.

There's a huge bulletin board outside the library on Main Street, so on my long walk home that night, I stopped to look it over.

There were only a few signs up that I hadn't seen before. The first was written in scratchy handwriting:

The Pumpkins Are Almost Ready.
Are You?

That one wasn't much help. I read the second sign:

MOSSGROVE'S ORANGE
CIRCUS IS IN TOWN! COME
SEE THE ASTONISHING ...

I groaned and moved on to the last sign:

Free Kitten. Orange Tabby.
Contact Mr. Banbury
(The Big Green House).

◉

As I stood outside the cave the next morning with an orange kitten in my arms, a big part of me wasn't sure if I was doing the right thing.

Like I said, there's just no way to predict how a cavegirl is going to react. Based on what she did to the stuffed tiger, I knew I'd have to be extra careful introducing the kitten to Kabungo.

But I worried for nothing. Because the second Kabungo saw the orange kitten ...

"Ya, ya! Targur! That! Me! Best try, Belly! Oh, Belly, best!"

I've still never seen Kabungo so excited.

41

She gave me about a dozen Grateful Cavegirl Squeezes (I survived). Then, as she took the kitten from me — so slowly and gently — she was just shaking with excitement. She was almost crying.

"What are you going to name him, K?" I said, wiping my eye.

"Huh?" She was hardly paying attention, she was so busy petting her new friend, who was purring like a refrigerator.

"Every tiger needs a name."

Kabungo looked straight up and bit her finger.

"Bun," she said finally.

"Bun?" I gave her a funny look.

"Ya."

"Why Bun, Kabungo?"

She bit her finger again. I'm shocked it doesn't have a hole in it.

"Dunno," she said, shrugging.

For a while, I thought maybe the kitten felt soft and warm like a fresh bun. But I doubt Kabungo even likes buns. I made her a cake once and she just sniffed it and said, "Blak!" She's more of a meat-and-bones cavegirl.

I gave Kabungo a long lecture about food and water and all the things tigers like. But she was so amazed and in love that all she said was, "Soft. Nice. Targur. Nice. Soft," over and over. So I decided to leave the two of them alone for a while.

After lunch, I went to check on them. As I got closer to the cave, though, I could hear a voice. It sounded like Kabungo was talking to someone.

I tiptoed into the cave.

And this is what I saw.

Kabungo was sitting by the fire, with Bun

on her lap and *Amazing A to Z* opened up on the floor in front of them. There were two bowls close by, one filled with water and one with some kind of meat. Kabungo was petting Bun and ... *reading* to him.

"C fir Cake, Bun," she said. "Blak. *Not* tasty."

She turned the page.

"D fir Drogon," she said. Actually, the D was for Dinosaur but that was pretty close. I was impressed.

"E fir ... Elphant. Shh Bun, kay? Not real. Shh. Safe cave, kay? Shh."

Bun purred.

Kabungo flipped the page.

And *I* tiptoed back into the sunlight.

THREE
Vibbles

EVERYONE HAS a favorite tree. Mine is the big bushy one in the middle of Lion's Park. It's better at making shade than any tree I've ever met. Sometimes I sit against it and read all afternoon.

One day I was reading under my tree when a leaf fluttered down and landed right at the end of Chapter Two.

"Miss VeDore," I whispered. Then I closed my book (leaves make perfect bookmarks) and headed home.

Falling leaves mean Halloween. Halloween

means pumpkins. And pumpkins, as everyone in Star City knows, mean Miss VeDore.

The tall house on Main Street that looks abandoned is actually Miss VeDore's house. It was a real live mansion once, according to my Uncle George. That was long before the paint flaked off, the chimney rotted like, well, a pumpkin, and the lawn grew up and decided it wanted to be a forest. The round window on the third floor has been broken for years. Once, I saw dark eyes sparkling in it.

Most people call Miss VeDore the Pumpkin Woman because she grows pumpkins and sells them. Most people are just a little bit frightened of her. In fact, there's only one person I know who isn't a bit scared of Miss VeDore — and she lives in a cave on Main Street.

I actually hadn't seen too much of Kabun-

go since she'd fallen in love with Bun. When people are in love, they act like they're in a snow globe. You can shake it as hard as you want, but they just go on floating and smiling.

Well, it's the same with cavegirls and kittens.

I thought I'd stop by the cave, though, just in case.

There was no answer when I banged a stone on the side of the cave, so I let myself in. Kabungo was so busy playing with the kitten — they were batting something around on the floor — that she didn't notice me for a whole minute.

"Oh Belly," she said finally, standing up. "Play?"

I couldn't quite see what they were playing with, it was so dark in the cave. At first I thought it was a mouse toy.

But no. It was ... a *mouse*.

"Umm, I'll pass," I said.

"Kay." Then she dove to the floor in time to snatch the mouse from Bun.

I didn't even bother to roll my eyes.

"Kabungo?" I said.

"Ya?" she said, getting up again, twirling the mouse around by its tail.

"Do you want to go with me to Miss Ve-Dore's?"

Kabungo lifted up her nose and squinted. That's her way of saying, "I require more information." So I told her that Miss VeDore was that *friendly* old woman in the big house on Main Street who had all the pumpkins.

Kabungo looked down and unsquinted. She had sufficient information.

"Nnn," she said, shaking her head. "Vibbles. Not tasty."

Call them vegetables or call them vibbles, Kabungo isn't a big fan. I explained to her that the pumpkin wouldn't be for eating and what a jack-o'-lantern was and how wonderful it would look on Halloween if she sat one in front of her cave.

Kabungo chewed her finger. She was thinking.

"Oh kay," she said finally, flinging the mouse into the corner. "Wego. Stay Bun kay?"

"Mi," Bun said, chasing after the mouse. I wasn't sure if that was a promise.

We had just left the cave when Kabungo darted around it into the bushes. I wondered what she was up to. A second later, she reappeared, dragging the rusty old wagon she uses to haul firewood.

"For vibbles," she said.

I nodded. I was impressed.

◉

It's always sunset at Miss VeDore's, even when the sun is high in the sky. That's because of the trees. There are just so many of them around her mansion and so many shadows that whenever you walk past 318 Main Street, it's like the sun slipped down the couch cushions.

It was just after lunch when we strolled up to Miss VeDore's. It was so dim and still, though, you'd swear it was after dinner. The only sounds were an owl hooting and the squealing of the wagon wheels.

I'm not a nervous person. But I was a little nervous just then.

The iron gate around Miss VeDore's mansion is locked almost every day of the year.

"Tasty meat," said Kabungo, taking a step forward. But I managed to drag her back to the path before anything drastic happened.

Miss VeDore had vanished. So we just kept following the path as it curved around the front of the house, the side and into the backyard.

Of course, it really wasn't what I'd call a backyard. It was more like one enormous pumpkin patch. There had to be a million pumpkins, from the size of my fist to the size of a dishwasher. There were vines growing and twisting around every tree and stone, like snakes. They even wound around an empty rocking chair in the middle of the garden. You couldn't have rocked it if you tried.

There was still no sign of Miss VeDore. There was a *sign* — a big wooden sign next to the rocking chair that said *Miss VeDore's*

Pumpkin Hollow, but its owner was nowhere in sight.

I told Kabungo that if we took our time picking out pumpkins, Miss VeDore was bound to show up sooner or later. Kabungo seemed to think that was a good idea. Right away, she went around sniffing and tapping on pumpkins, like those strange people in the supermarket.

Choosing a pumpkin was harder than I expected. They were all great. A few were so big you could live in them. One looked just like my Aunt Ev.

Finally, I saw one that seemed to have "me" carved all over it. It was skinny and intelligent-looking and not too big.

I twisted it off the vine. Then I went to find Kabungo.

But there was no sign of her now, either. I

looked behind every pumpkin, the sign, under the chair.

I called her.

The only answer was the vine leaves rustling in the breeze.

When I get nervous, it's like there's a large spider in my stomach that's trying hard to climb out.

Well, when I couldn't find Kabungo, the spider in my stomach was enormous. It was a tarantula. I told myself that I was overreacting. Kabungo was probably fine and not doing anything crazy.

Then I remembered the raccoon.

As I raced back down the path, I heard a loud squeaking. I wasn't sure what sound a raccoon would make if it was wrestling with a cavegirl, but I ran even faster, just in case.

When I got to the front door, there was no raccoon — and no Kabungo.

The door, though, was open wide. As it blew back and forth, it squealed.

Somewhere deep in the mansion, a glass smashed.

Somewhere deep in my stomach, a spider scurried.

I didn't want to go inside. But I knew I had to.

I took a deep breath, swallowed spider legs and slipped through the front door ...

◉

One of the questions on my last English test was *What is boredom? Define boredom in one sentence.*

My answer was *Boredom is when everything turns out like you expected.* Ms. Beaux-Beaux

put a big fat X by my answer and wrote, *Incorrect. Boredom is an emotional state characterized by a feeling of disinterest.*

When I read that, I experienced boredom. Because that's exactly the kind of thing I *expected* her to write.

When I stepped through Miss VeDore's front door, I expected to see mice, spider webs and bats flying out of the fireplace like sparks.

What I did see, though, was a lot more exciting. Because it surprised me.

When you're best friends with a cavegirl, believe me, you're not easily surprised.

On the outside, Miss VeDore's mansion was — crumbly. It was dusty. It was like a cookie that looked just wonderful till you dropped it on the carpet.

On the inside, Miss VeDore's mansion was

— lovely. It was clean and fancy. Everything in it was wooden, antique-looking, shining. The orange walls were covered in pictures and paintings. Next to the staircase, a grandfather clock ticked. There was even a chandelier.

The whole place reminded me of that Peter, Peter, Pumpkin Eater poem, where the wife lived in a pumpkin house. Only this was more like a pumpkin mansion.

I was admiring a tall painting of an ostrich, when my foot touched something.

It was a bowl of cat food. I wondered where the cat was.

A breeze blew my hair. It was coming, I was sure, from upstairs.

I decided to investigate. I walked up the staircase ...

The second floor wasn't at all like the first floor. It was darker. And dustier. The wall-

paper was peeling. There was a long hallway with closed doors that I'm guessing were bedrooms.

The breeze wasn't a breeze anymore. It was just plain wind. It was rushing and sunlight was pouring through an open door at the end of the dark hallway.

I moved closer to the doorway. The wind grew stronger. I peeked through the door.

I gasped. I gasped again. I don't double-gasp very often. Only when I see something that makes me think I need glasses.

On the other side of the doorway was a balcony, a veranda. On the veranda was a white table. And sitting at the table, drinking tea, eating biscuits and *chatting*, were Miss VeDore and Kabungo.

I'd never seen my cave friend looking so civilized. She wasn't holding the teacup

properly (she was wearing it on her finger like a ring) and she was spilling a lot and drinking too fast. But still, I was impressed. I was surprised, too, that she could be so talkative.

She was telling Miss VeDore about Bun.

"Bun targur no no night sleep targur no run Bun no Bun bad targur bad soft niiice."

Between the words "sleep" and "tiger," somehow she swallowed a biscuit and half a cup of tea.

On the other side of the table, Miss VeDore was sitting there nodding like she completely understood.

Maybe she did.

While I was spying on them, kind of wondering what Kabungo would say next, Miss VeDore looked up and said in her whispery way, "Have a seat, dear. And ... some tea?"

Just because you're spying on people

doesn't mean you're invisible. I'll have to remember that.

I stepped into the sunlight.

"Oh Belly hi," said Kabungo, smiling, her teeth full of crumbs.

"Why did you run off?" I said.

"Thirsty," was all she said, downing the rest of her tea and grabbing another biscuit. I was shocked that she even liked them. You learn new things about a cavegirl every day.

"It was *I* who ran off, dear," said Miss VeDore. "To fetch ... *refreshments*." She smiled a jack-o'-lantern smile. Miss VeDore poured out some tea and passed me a biscuit. I nibbled on it and felt a bit more comfortable. Biscuits are like that.

"Nice baskets!" said Kabungo.

Miss VeDore smiled. She sat there smiling

and Kabungo sat there eating and I sat there wondering what to say.

"Halloween's coming," I said finally.

"Really?" said Miss VeDore, sounding surprised.

"In a few weeks," I said, sounding even more surprised.

Miss VeDore shook her head.

"Sooner than you think," she whispered. "Halloween is coming ... now."

She pointed at the doorway.

I looked behind me. I didn't know what she was talking about. I couldn't hear anything or see anything.

Miss VeDore kept pointing — and staring — at the door.

"Halloween," she repeated, "is coming."

I swallowed. I think I had goosebumps.

"Halloween ... is ... *almost* ... here."

I glanced at Kabungo. She was too busy wolfing down the last biscuit, though, to be paying attention.

"There!" cried Miss VeDore suddenly, standing up. "Halloween! Halloween! Halloween!"

As I turned to look where Miss VeDore was pointing, I decided that if nothing was there and Miss VeDore was as crazy as everyone in town said she was, I'd just get up, grab Kabungo and run.

But something was there. And it was stepping out of the shadows.

It was ... the *raccoon*. He trotted across the veranda like he owned it and hopped onto Miss VeDore's lap.

"Where have you been, Halloween?" she said, petting him. "Silly boy. Getting into mischief?"

The raccoon squeaked. Kabungo finally looked up — the words "tasty meat" popped into my head — but all she did was rub the crumbs off her face and say, "Oh too full. Later kay?"

"You have a raccoon named Halloween?" I asked.

"Isn't he darling?" whispered Miss Ve-Dore.

He *was* kind of handsome, for a raccoon. His fur was pretty shiny. He even had a green collar.

Suddenly, I understood why there was cat food but no cat. I remembered those sparkling dark eyes in the window ...

Miss VeDore gave Halloween the rest of her biscuit. He held it in both hands and nibbled on it without spilling a crumb. Then she poured a bit of tea onto her saucer and let

Halloween lap it up daintily, like a cat.

I looked at Kabungo — there was either a tea stain or a bit of biscuit on every inch of her — and sighed.

"Well," I said, getting up, "we'd better pay for our pumpkins. After all," I glanced at the raccoon. "Halloween is here."

"Hmm?" said Miss VeDore, looking puzzled. "Oh, no, no, dear. Not yet. Not for a few weeks."

FOUR
Fundersticks

YOU CAN USUALLY see a storm coming from
a mile off. It's big and noisy and takes its time
about things, like my Uncle Al.

But sometimes a storm pops in unexpect-
edly, like my Aunt Ev.

That's how *this* storm was ...

It was a beautiful fall day — the warmest
in weeks. As usual, I was on my way to Kabungo's.

I knocked on the side of the cave. A pair
of green eyes squinted in the dark. A pair of
nostrils twitched.

"Oh hi Belly come," she said at last, once she figured out it was me and not a wild elephant.

Deep in the cave, the fire was blazing. Something orange and fuzzy lay spread out on one side of the fire, purring. Bun. Something flat and green lay spread out on the other side.

"K?" I said. "What *is* that?"

Kabungo looked left, then right.

"Skin," she said.

Though Kabungo isn't easily shocked, she *is* easily shocking.

"What ... kind of skin?" I felt I had to ask.

"Sillymunder," she said. I didn't doubt it. But I did change the subject.

"Have you thought of a Halloween costume yet?" I asked.

"Nnn," she said, sitting down.

I couldn't be too angry with her. I hadn't thought of one yet, either.

I was about to suggest Frankenstein when I was interrupted — by thunder.

Kabungo perked up like a dog. She raced out of the cave.

Before I could wonder where she'd gone or what she was up to, she raced full speed back into the cave, dragging a big branch behind her.

I watched as she cracked it into about a hundred pieces. Then she sat down and started drawing something in the floor dust with her finger. To me it just looked like a circle with a couple of lines beside it. To Kabungo, though, it had to mean something important. She was biting down on her tongue like it was for dinner.

I didn't ask, "What on earth are you up to

now?" Because I knew she'd never hear me. She was far away, deep in her cavegirl brain. All I could do was wait for her to come back out.

While I waited, I straightened up the cave a bit. My friend lives a pretty simple life. The only thing she has a lot of is dust. Bun didn't make my job any easier. He kept swirling around my legs and rolling over one step ahead of me.

A cat's mission in life is to trip you, so it has something warm and soft to lie on.

I was just finishing up, when Kabungo pulled her tongue back in. She breathed in. She closed her eyes. She opened them. She had the strangest, calmest look in her face, like she was about to say the wisest thing of her life.

"Soffft," she said.

I waited. If this was her big chance to say something deep, I wanted her to have all the time she needed.

My friend nodded proudly. She looked down at her drawing and then back up at me.

"Soffft," was all she said, again (oh, well). And then she jumped up and — grabbed onto my hair. Gently. She smoothed it down like it was a kitten.

"Belly hair soft nice Belly."

It's true. My hair is soft. I shampoo every day.

"Belly?"

"Yes, K?"

"Have soft, Belly? Little nice have Belly some?"

I raised my eyebrows.

"You want some of my *hair*, Kabungo?"

"Ya ya."

I took Kabungo's hand and removed it from my head.

"I have a better idea, K. My hair *is* soft. But *cotton* is softer."

"*More* soft?" said Kabungo, her big eyes getting even bigger.

I nodded.

"And if you want," I said, "I'll get you some. I have to go to Gobshaw's anyway. For batteries." Flashlights like to play dead, I've found, whenever there's a storm.

Kabungo chewed on her finger to show she was considering it.

Finally, she gave me the Cavegirl Signal of Approval. She grunted.

◉

Of course, the second I stepped into Gobshaw's Drug Shop — a bell jingles when you

open the door — Mr. Gobshaw jumped up
and said, "Welcome! We have everything!"

"But do you have six C-cell batteries?" I
asked.

"Yup!" he said. "They're next to the ham-
ster food."

Of course, he was right. Mr. Gobshaw has
a system. And the cotton batten (I couldn't
forget that) was next to the fortune cookies.

"Big storm coming," said Mr. Gobshaw,
tapping away on the cash register.

"I know."

"*Really* big," he said, giving me my change.

"I kind of like storms," I said.

"Ditto," said Mr. Gobshaw. "Nothing
freshens a place up like the roof blowing off.
It's a little musty in here anyway, don't you
think?"

Mr. Gobshaw's sense of humor is —

different. That's actually fine with me. I like different.

I was just about to step outside when Mr. Gobshaw said, "Beverly? Oh, Beverly?"

I get so used to being called "Belly" that sometimes I don't recognize my own name.

"Don't forget. Next week umbrellas are 50 percent off!"

"But . . . it won't be storming anymore," I said, puzzled.

"Exactly," said Mr. Gobshaw, winking.

◉

By the time I got back to the cave, the dark clouds were hovering right over Star City. The wind was picking up fast. It was thundering a lot now. The storm wasn't just coming, it was *here*.

The storm was here. But Kabungo wasn't.

You can't take your eyes off a cavegirl, not for a minute.

"Kabungo?" I called.

In the corner of the cave, a pile of blankets quivered.

"Oh, Kabungo," I said, reaching out.

"Go, elphant!" said the pile of blankets.

I sighed.

"It's *me*, K."

The blankets stopped quivering. One big eye peeked out of one very small hole.

"Oh hi Belly," said my friend, throwing off the blankets. "Have softer?"

I handed her the bag of cotton. In about three seconds, she'd ripped it open and dumped it on the floor next to the pile of sticks. That's when Bun decided he'd be a very *helpful kitty* by batting them all over the cave.

"Bad! Bad! Bad! No! Not! Bun! Baaad tar-gur!"

Cats are good listeners, but they're *brilliant* ignorers. So I had no choice but to pick him up and hold him until Kabungo was finished doing whatever she was doing.

I watched her pull two sticks out of the pile that were a bit shorter and sturdier than the rest. She wound the cotton around and around one end of each till they looked like something a giant might clean his ears with.

"Fundersticks," she said, frowning seriously.

"Mmm hmm," I said.

Next she carefully arranged the other sticks into — it kind of reminded me of a log cabin, only much smaller. Instead of putting a roof on it, she pulled a needle out of her pouch, stitched the lizard skins into one big piece and

stretched it over the top of the structure.

"Funderdrum," she said, even more seriously.

I laughed. *Of course.* A drum. *Drumsticks.*

Kabungo had built herself a musical instrument. I was impressed.

Kabungo picked up the fundersticks. But before she could test out her creation, there was a VERY LOUD THUNDERCLAP.

Bun jumped out of my arms and under the table. Kabungo clamped onto my leg like a boa constrictor. So I explained — we'd just learned about it in science class — how lightning is caused by the friction of water droplets and how thunder is just the sound of hot air expanding. But I could tell she wasn't paying attention. The thought cloud above Kabungo's head was not full of water droplets. It was full of big gray elephants, stampeding.

Another thunderclap. *Another.* I was sure I'd have Kabungo wrapped around my legs until the storm passed.

But then something happened. Something ... unexpected. I'm not sure where she got

the courage — it was thundering louder than ever — but she suddenly let go of my legs, picked up her drumsticks and started drumming. And while she drummed, she ...

Well, she didn't quite sing, but something close to it. I guess you could call it poetry.

> *Bungofunder*
> *drum*
> *drum*
> *ELPHANTS GO!*

> *Funder funder*
> *drum*
> *drum*
> *BAD BAD ELPHANTS BAD BAD*
> *BAD BAD GO!*

(I didn't say it was very *good* poetry.)

The louder it thundered, the louder Kabungo sang and the harder she banged her drum, until I couldn't tell one from the other and I had to plug my ears to keep *their* drums from shattering.

The lightning flashed and the wind thrashed. And still she kept drumming, singing at the top of her lungs, her big black tiger eyes twinkling.

And then ...

The lightning stopped. The wind died down. The thunder faded away.

The storm was over.

Kabungo put down her drumsticks. Bun crawled out from under the table, looking perfectly calm.

"Mrr mrrr," he said. Then he curled up on Kabungo's lap and purred.

"See, Belly?" said my friend. "Safe. Belly

safe gone. *Chicken* elphants."

The only thing I could think to say was, "Oh, Kabungo."

We stepped outside. The clouds had scattered. The sky above Star City was full of stars.

"Big Dumper," said Kabungo proudly, pointing up. Lately I'd been trying to teach her about astronomy. It was harder than you could ever imagine.

I didn't correct my friend. There are times for teaching and times for tipping your head back and laughing.

Just then, it was one of those laughing times.

FIVE
Himplepotamus

KABUNGO, BUN and I were sitting by the fire one afternoon. Bun was stretched out on my friend's lap, purring. *Amazing A to Z* was stretched out on mine.

Kabungo had actually been doing really well up to that point. She now knew all of her letters and most of the words in the book. She was even pronouncing them correctly. "Without proper pronunciation," Ms. Beaux-Beaux likes to say, "words are just *bird chatter.*"

One letter, though, still stumped Kabungo.

"Come on," I said. "You *know* this."

"Mmm," she said, sticking her finger in her mouth.

"It's …"

My friend looked at me with Confuddled Cavegirl Eyes.

"It's *H*," I said. "*H*."

"Ohhh ya kay Belly," she said.

I took a deep breath.

"And H is for …"

Kabungo chewed on her finger like gum. Her eyes brightened.

"Humplemoose?"

"*Hippopotamus*."

"Ya dat said. Humplemoose."

"No, K," I said. "Not quite. Hip-po-pot-a-mus."

"Dat said Belly! HUMPLEMOOSE!"

"You're not *listening*, Kabungo! Hip-po-potamus!"

"HUMPLEMOOSE, HUMPLEMOOSE, HUMPLEMOOSE!" she cried, pounding her fists on the floor.

"Hippo —"

"Yak, yak, yak," said Kabungo. She picked up Bun and lay flat on her back.

"If you want to learn your alphabet, Kabungo, you have to have a little more —"

"Yak, yak, yak," she said again, trying to kiss her squirming kitty.

I didn't bother to say "patience," because I'd lost mine.

I snapped the book shut. I stood up.

"Wherego?" she said, jumping up, too.

"Anywhere else," I said.

"Ohh kay. Kabungo come?"

"Definitely *not*," I said.

She followed me to the mouth of the cave.

"Pleasing, Belly?" she said.

"No thanks," I said. "Not till you start acting a little more civilized."

I stormed off. After I'd crossed the street, I glanced back at the cave.

A pair of sad cavegirl eyes sparkled in the dark.

◉

Apologizing sounds easy. It *should* be. It should be the easiest thing in history to go up to someone and say, "I'm sorry."

It isn't. Apologies are heavy. They're *boulders*. It's hard work pushing a boulder, even if it's just across the room. A lot of people give up halfway and lose a friend forever.

I didn't want that to happen to Kabungo and me.

So the next day, I pointed myself in the direction of the cave and started pushing.

It wasn't easy. But I did it anyway.

I was just about to cross Main Street when I noticed the head of a cavegirl pop out of the cave — and then the rest of her. She glanced left and right, then took off sneakily down the street.

I picked up speed and followed her.

I knew it wasn't any of my business. I probably shouldn't have gone after her, but my feet did anyway. Feet aren't always reasonable.

Besides, Kabungo was wearing her beast furs and her snakeskin pouch. That usually meant trouble.

Following Kabungo wasn't easy. She's naturally suspicious and never took three steps without looking over her shoulder at least

once. Luckily, there was always a mailbox or a friendly person I could duck behind.

Now, if it was Kabungo following me, all she'd have to do is follow my scent. She's like a bloodhound.

My sense of smell may not be that great, but my sense of snoop is *amazing*.

Pretty soon we were on the outskirts of town. I followed her for another mile down the road. Then she turned onto another road, looked slyly all around her (I jumped into the ditch) and slipped into the trees.

There isn't a forest on the edge of town, exactly, but something like a forest, a small one called Hazelwood. Parents tell kids it's haunted so they stay out of it.

When I saw Kabungo go into the woods, I wondered what she was up to. She didn't have her bow and arrow, so she couldn't be hunting.

I wondered if I was brave enough to find out ...

I decided I was. My fear of not figuring something out is stronger than my fear of ghosts.

Tracking Kabungo through the woods was even harder. The trees were mostly too skinny to hide behind. It was only a week till Halloween, and the leaves had all dropped off, so I needed to step at exactly the same time as Kabungo to disguise the crunching.

There were a couple of close calls. I had to drop down to the ground once, like I'd been shot at. But on the whole it went about as smoothly as following a cavegirl can.

When it looked like Kabungo had suddenly sunk into the ground, I knew my friend had either stepped in quicksand or run downhill.

I picked up my pace.

It was a hill, thank goodness, a pretty steep one. At the bottom, there was one little dead tree and a heap of mud. But no Kabungo.

At first I was mad at myself. A cavegirl is a slippery animal. If you want to catch one, you

can't afford to lose sight of her for a second.

Then I was nervous. Maybe, I thought, Kabungo stepped in that deep mud and sank down like a woolly mammoth.

Then I was just scared. It would be dark soon and with no Kabungo to follow, I wasn't sure if I could even find my way back out of the woods.

"Kabungo?" I called out. At this point I didn't care how angry she would be. I just wanted out of that place.

Except for the wind blowing around the leaves, though, there was no reply.

I kept walking. *She couldn't have gone far*, I kept telling myself, as I walked up the next hill.

After about a half hour of wandering around calling my friend's name, I heard something.

It wasn't a cavegirl. It wasn't a ghost. It was more like ... a *tiger*. I mean, a deep, growling sound like a tiger might make. And it was *right behind me*.

My heart raced, and so did I. Even though it was getting harder to see — wherever the sun was, it had to be setting — I ran as hard as possible, dodging rocks and trees. I ran till I just about dropped dead and then I *did* drop but only because I tripped on a log or something.

I curled up like a hedgehog, expecting to be devoured at any second.

But nothing happened. After a few minutes, I uncurled myself. I sat up. I stood up. I took a big breath. I looked behind me ...

Nothing was there. But, no. There was something. Not a tiger or any animal but ...

A light.

I walked towards it. The light got brighter.

It was coming from the window of a small house, a cabin. The window glowed orange like a jack-o'-lantern. Smoke rose from the chimney.

As I got close to the cabin, I could hear a deep voice coming from inside. I got down on my hands and knees, crawled up to the window, then slowly poked my head up till I could see inside.

I saw a fireplace and a crackling fire. I saw an old man in an armchair on one side of the fire and an old dog in a basket on the other.

And sitting on the floor between them, with her legs crossed, was Kabungo, grinning.

I was so happy to see her that I just about tapped on the glass. But then I remembered that the whole point of snooping is not to be seen. So I crouched there, watching and listening ...

The old man started talking again, but his voice was so low that I still couldn't make it out. I had no trouble, though, making out what Kabungo said.

"Ha ha, Grandpa!" she laughed, slapping her knees. "Funny!"

If my friend had glanced out the window just then, she would have seen me looking stunned.

I didn't know she had a grandpa, or *any* family.

The old man said something else. Kabungo tipped backwards with laughter, right into the basket. The big dog growled at her, but she just put her arm around him and guffawed. He growled twice as loud then. At first I thought there would be a fight.

But he wasn't growling at Kabungo.

He lifted his head. He sniffed the air.

"Hmm?" said Kabungo. "Hmm, dog? Meat? Meat?" Now Kabungo lifted her head and started sniffing.

The big dog barked — and looked right at the window.

"Uh-oh," I thought, ducking down.

A few seconds later, I heard the front door open.

"Thisway, dog?" said Kabungo.

As they came around the one side of the house, I ran as quietly as I could to the other side.

"Oh thatway?" The dog must have changed directions. I ran back to where I'd started.

The big dog barked.

"What, dog? More thisway? Oh kay."

This went on for a long time.

Finally, one of them — I'm not sure if it was Kabungo or the dog — had a brainwave

and decided that if one of them went *one* way and one went the *other* way, they would catch me for sure.

Which is just what happened.

"Grrr," said the dog.

"Oh hi, Belly," said Kabungo. She didn't even look surprised. She grabbed me by the hand.

"Come," she said. "Meet Grandpa."

She dragged me around the house, through the front door and right up to the old man.

"Grandpa? Belly. Belly, *hi*."

"Umm … hi," I said.

The old man smiled. There was a stool next to his chair with a tray on it. He picked up the tray — it was covered with strange-smelling cheeses — and held it out to us.

Of course Kabungo grabbed a piece. I took

one, too, to be polite, but slipped it into my pocket.

The old man waved his hands like he wanted us both to sit down.

Kabungo jumped back into the basket with the dog and wrapped her arms around it. I decided to sit in front of the basket. Quite a bit in front. I was less scared of the old man than I was of the old dog. Old men growl, but they usually don't bite.

The old guy started talking, only he mumbled so badly, I couldn't understand him. So I looked around the room for a bit. That was hard, too, since the cabin was on the dark side. Aside from the fire, there were no lights or lamps.

I could make out a few things, though. Behind the old man, in the one corner, was a stuffed bear. It was a *real* stuffed bear. I

mean, a bear that had been stuffed. Its eyes twinkled in the firelight. I tried not to look at them.

In the other corner there was an even bigger basket, way too big for the dog. I couldn't see a bed anywhere. I wondered if the basket was where the old man slept.

Of course I took a good look at the man, too. He was wearing a strange kind of green hat with long ear flaps. His whole face was sunburned except for around his eyes. He looked a bit like a raccoon.

That was about all I could tell from looking, so I tried listening again.

"Het was een koude winter," he said, folding his hands.

"Ha ha!" said Kabungo. I gave her a funny look. The only word I really caught was "winter." I listened a bit harder.

"Een ʒeer koude winter," he went on, shaking his head seriously.

"Ha ha ha!" laughed Kabungo.

I still didn't get it. I leaned forward. I listened as hard as I could.

"Een ʒeeeer, ʒeeeer koude winter."

That's when the lightbulb in my head blinked on.

The old man wasn't mumbling at all. In fact, he was speaking loud and clear. The reason I couldn't understand his English was because it *wasn't* English. I had no idea what language it was.

I really doubted that Kabungo, who barely spoke English, understood a word of this mystery language.

As I looked back and forth from my friend to her "grandpa," I realized that I'd never been in a stranger situation in my life.

When you're best friends with a cavegirl, that's saying quite a bit.

"*Mijn broer en ik hadden honger.*"

"Ha ha, Grandpa! Sooo funny!"

I turned around and gave Kabungo another strange look. I give her strange looks so often, though, she probably stopped noticing a long time ago.

The old man went on, waving his hands as he spoke.

"*Ik zag een patrijs. Een bruine patrijs.*"

Kabungo rolled back out of the basket with laughter. The dog looked relieved.

"'*Oh, broer!' zei Christofoor. 'Wat een geluk!*'"

Kabungo got up and staggered across the room, holding her stomach and laughing.

"*We hadden onze pistolen. Bang! Bang!*"

I had to jump up then and grab Kabungo or

she would have stumbled right into the fire. But then we both tipped over and knocked the cheese tray off the stool and all over the floor. I picked up a few pieces — Kabungo wolfed down a few more — and I helped her back to her basket. She was safer with the dog.

"*'Ach!' Ik huilde. 'Christofoor, je slaagt mijn schoen!'* "

Kabungo flopped right back *out* of the basket, laughing, her mouth full of cheese.

"*'Broer!' riep Christofoor. 'Je slaagt mijn hoed!'* "

"Oooh," she groaned. "Tooo funny, Grandpa!"

"*We lachten de hele weg naar huis. We hadden tomatensoep.*"

I *jumped*, because someone knocked on the door. Actually, it was more like a scratch. A *big* scratch. The hair on my neck stood up,

though the hair on Kabungo's neck (she has a lot of it) looked fine. The dog didn't seem to care either. Not even when there was another, bigger scratch and a sound — a deep growly sound that sounded awfully familiar.

"Dat is Nikolaas," said the old man, getting out of his armchair. He walked across the room — he was so tall he had to duck — and opened the door.

And in stepped ...

A MOUNTAIN LION.

"Eyes are liars," my Uncle George once told me. "Don't believe a word they say." So at first, I didn't. But when I rubbed my eyes and I could *still* see a mountain lion and I could hear it purring like a house cat as it trotted across the room? Well, I had no choice but to believe.

I remembered the growling sound I'd

heard in the woods earlier and shivered from head to toe.

"Nice targur!" said Kabungo, nodding.

The big cat purred, rubbed up against the old man's leg, then sat down in front of the fire. I wanted to jump through the window but thought it would be safer just to sit perfectly still and not make too many sounds.

Before he sat down again, the old man held out the plate, even though the cheese was now covered with dog hair. Kabungo grabbed another slice. I just shook my head.

Grandpa kept talking — something about Christofoor, I think, and a ham sandwich — and then yawned more and more and finally shut his eyes. The mountain lion, meanwhile, had curled up in the big basket in the corner. I'm not sure which one snored louder.

"Umm, Kabungo?" I said. "I think we'd better go."

"Hmm?" said Kabungo, picking some dog hair out of her teeth. "Oh kay Belly."

Even though it was pitch dark out now, my friend had no trouble finding her way through the woods and back into town. In fact, she skipped along like it was daylight. It was all I could do to keep up with her.

"*That* was your grandpa?" I gasped, out of breath, at the mouth of the cave.

"Ya," was all she said.

It was too late — and I was too tired — to ask her any more questions just then. We said our goodnights.

As I walked away ...

"Belly?" said my friend.

I turned back and received a Crushing Cavegirl Hug.

"Kabungo sore," she said, squeezing her hardest. I was pretty sure she meant "sorry."

"I'm sorry, too, Kabungo," I managed to say at last.

The boulder broke up and turned to dust.

"Himplepotamus," Kabungo whispered in my ear, before letting me go.

"Himplepotamus," I whispered back.

SIX
Flimsy Tree

THERE ARE TWO kinds of research: the kind you do at the library and the kind you do by sticking your nose into other people's business.

I like the second kind best.

One Saturday, I was sitting in Lion's Park under my favorite tree doing one kind of research — reading *Life in Prehistoric Times*.

I was just starting a new chapter when something caught my eye. At first I thought it was a cat.

It wasn't a cat. It was a Kabungo. Tiptoeing. She tiptoed to a tree on the far side of the park, looked left and right ... then climbed it like a lumberjack.

"It's time," I thought, shutting my book, "for the other kind of research."

Before I could take a step, something else caught my eye. At first, again, I thought it was a cat.

It *was* a cat. It was Bun. He scampered up the trunk, like nothing.

I'm not very good at climbing trees. But curiosity is a cat. When I crept up to Kabungo's tree, my curiosity shot straight up it. And *I* held on as tightly as I could.

I scraped my elbow and my left cheek and both my knees. But I made it up the tree in one piece.

I pushed aside some leaves. Above me there was a big V in the middle of the tree where the two main arms branched off. Kabungo was standing in the middle of the V, muttering to herself. There was no sign of Bun.

I climbed just a little higher. Now I could hear what my friend was saying. I held on tight to the tree trunk, peeked through the leaves and listened.

It wasn't eavesdropping. It was research.

"Oh Mom hi Mom," it sounded like Kabungo said.

That can't be right, I thought. I kept listening.

"Oh Dad hi Dad," it seemed like she said next.

That can't be right, either. As far as I knew

— I didn't think the old man in the woods counted — Kabungo had no family.

Of course, if she did have a family, it wouldn't have surprised me at all to learn that they lived in a tree.

I leaned forward. I squinted. I couldn't see anyone. Unless a whole tribe of cavepeople was hiding quietly in the leaves, my friend was talking to herself.

Just then, in fact, she seemed to be hugging a big branch.

Kabungo hugs are powerful. It must have been a very strong branch.

"Big brudder!" she cried now, letting go and slapping a twig she must have brushed against. "Bad! Not scratch no!"

I raised my eyebrows. This was getting ridiculous.

"Baaad brudder," she said, shaking her finger.

It took all of my might not to laugh. Luckily, my friend put her Basic Cavegirl Face back on, bounced over to another branch and threw her arms around *it*.

"Sitter!" she said. "Oh small sitter miss much Kabungo. Nice sitter soft sitter soffft ..." She stroked the tree bark like it was a kitten.

Very carefully, I raised my eyebrows even higher. And then Kabungo raised *hers*. Because she'd noticed something.

Not me, fortunately, but something on her arm. Squinting hard, I could just barely see the faintest scratch from where she'd brushed against the twig.

"Ooooh," she said now, frowning and letting go of the branch. She jumped back to the

other side of the tree.

"BAD BRUDDER BIG KABUNGO BIG BAD *BAD!*"

I'd never seen my friend so angry. She *snapped* the twig off the branch, cracked it over her knee and chucked the pieces to the ground.

If Kabungo had a real brother, I'd definitely feel sorry for him.

"Oh come Mom!" she called out. "I'm come!" She tossed the leaves over her shoulder — they plopped on my lap — and went back to the "mother" branch. I examined the leaves. They were in pretty rough shape after all that sisterly affection.

If Kabungo had an actual baby sister, I'd feel sorry for her, too.

For about another ten minutes, as I clung there huddling in the leaves, I watched Ka-

bungo jump from one branch to another, chatting, kissing, kicking and fighting with them, like … well, like a real family.

I know I say this a lot, but it really was the strangest thing.

Strange but also … kind of sad.

I don't know a lot about Kabungo. In fact, no one in Star City has a clue who she is or where she comes from. To most people she's just that strange kid who lives in a cave on Main Street.

I want to learn more about her, to *research*, but it's so hard. You can't just go to the library and look under "K" for Kabungo. I wish I could.

I decided the best thing at that point was to climb back down the tree as quietly as I could. The longer I stayed, the more likely it was that she'd spot me, and I know that when

I'm caught talking to myself, I'm mortified.

Besides, my arms were numb.

I'd just started my way down, when something landed on my head. Something heavy.

"Purr," said the heavy something.

Cats have a special talent for disappearing when you *do* want them and then reappearing when you *don't*. My Aunt Ev calls it Cat Magic. She has eleven cats and they're all magicians.

"Mi. Purrrr."

"Shh," I said as quietly as I could. Unfortunately, "shh" is the one word cats don't understand.

"MEOW," said Bun.

"*Quiet*," I whispered. I reached up to grab him, but he only dug his claws into my scalp.

"OW!" I screamed, sounding a lot like a

cat myself.

Kabungo whirled around. Bun jumped off my head and dashed up to his master.

"Belly!" she cried. Her big eyes got twice as big. Luckily, she has a very large head. Her expression was so strange that I wasn't sure if she was about to pelt me with acorns or start bawling.

"Oh oh Belly umm Kabungo …" (She only calls herself Kabungo when she thinks she's in trouble.) "Belly Belly umm Kabungo umm …"

"It's all right, K."

She hung her head. I could tell she was embarrassed. As I stared at her big cavegirl eyes, I realized I'd never seen my friend look so small and sad before.

"Kabungo?" I said.

She looked up.

"Kabungo ... is this ... your *family* tree?"

Kabungo's eyes brightened. She stood up straight.

"Ya ya!" she said. "Good you, Belly! Flimsy tree! Kabungo's flimsy tree!"

She jumped down from her branch onto mine. The whole tree shook. Bun pounced to the ground and chased the falling acorns.

"Good you, Belly!" she said again, giving me her Happy Cavegirl Hug. (It's like a bear hug, only more ferocious.)

"Oh Belly," she said, her head still on my shoulder. "Belly know. Belly know flimsy Kabungo."

For a second I thought I felt something damp on my shoulder. I wasn't sure. I thought ... but no. Cavegirls don't cry. Though they do sometimes drool.

Before we left the park, I retrieved my

copy of *Life in Prehistoric Times*. Even though I was only on the third chapter, I took it back to the library the next day.

There are some kinds of research you just can't do with books.

SEVEN
Hopping Bird Day

DEFINE *"unexpected."*

That was one of the questions on my last English test.

I wrote, *The unexpected is what happens three times a day at least.*

When I got my test back the next day, there was a big fat X next to my answer.

Obviously, Ms. Beaux-Beaux had never met Kabungo.

One time, when I stepped into the cave, I found my friend spread out like a cloth on the table, fast asleep. Another time, she and Bun

and a bullfrog were running around the cave so fast I couldn't tell who was chasing who.

I think I understand the meaning of "unexpected" better than anyone.

One Saturday morning, I knocked on the cave.

"COME BELLY!" yelled my friend from deep inside. She'd grown a little more trusting lately.

I walked in … and tripped on something. When I looked down, I saw a moose staring up at me from the floor.

Luckily, it was just the head, and it was stuffed. One of the antlers was missing. A moose only needs one antler, though, to trip you.

Of course I was relieved that it wasn't a real head, but only a little. I've always found stuffed animal heads creepy. Maybe

it's the fake eyes, but it might be the very real teeth.

I'm not the only one, either. In the farthest corner of the cave, Bun was puffed up like a porcupine. I don't know if porcupines hiss, but kittens sure do.

Kabungo helped me up. I was about to ask her where on earth she had found a moose head, but didn't bother. It was Saturday. It's always too early to argue on a Saturday.

When I came back the next day, there was a cracked fish tank sitting on her table. At least there were no fish because there was no water in it, either.

Bun was curled up inside the tank, purring. He probably felt safe in there, from the moose.

But when I dropped by the day after that and discovered my friend sitting on a three-

legged chair, wearing a torn sombrero, I knew I couldn't keep quiet anymore.

"K? Where are you getting all this stuff?"

My friend sank her head between her shoulders like a turtle and looked guilty.

"*K?* You're not stealing again, are you? Like with the teeth?" My Uncle George still keeps his teeth under lock and key.

Kabungo shook her head. At the same time, she sank her head even deeper and looked *twice* as guilty.

"And you're not digging in people's trash cans, I hope? Remember what Officer Barney said?"

Kabungo chewed her finger for a bit.

Finally, she shook her head. She'd never looked guiltier, though, in her life.

I put my hands on my hips.

"I don't think you're being honest with

me," I said, sounding a lot like my mother.

That's when Kabungo stopped looking guilty and started looking *angry*.

"Wronging Belly not! Stealing? Wrong tongue! Baaad Belly!"

I told her I didn't believe her. She jumped up and down. I told her I *still* didn't believe her. That only made her angrier.

Kabungo and I don't fight that often, but when we do, it's always BIG.

It all ended with Kabungo screaming (it was her trademark Raging Cavegirl Ruckus), kicking the moose head — the other antler went flying off — and yelling, "Go Belly go go GO!"

So I did. If the cave had a door, I would have slammed it.

◉

I didn't sleep very well that night …

About a minute after the sun came up I heard a sound. It was like a quiet grinding or scratching. I slipped into my slippers and crept downstairs.

My mom wasn't up yet, so I knew the noise wasn't breakfast. I stood on the bottom step and listened.

Scratch, scratch, scratch.

It was coming from the front door.

I crept closer. I looked out the window.

I didn't see anyone.

I waited a minute. I opened the front door.

There was no one in sight. No one, that is, but Bun, who was curled up on the doormat, purring.

"Mif!" he said.

I bent down to pet him, and noticed some-

thing. It was a dirty old shoe. Underneath the shoe was a piece of paper.

I picked it up and examined it. Something was scribbled all over it in charcoal.

I flipped the paper over. The only thing on the other side was a familiar-looking picture of an elephant with a large letter "E" next to it.

That made me angry all over again. Kabungo was so close to knowing her alphabet now — she kept getting stuck on "X for Xylophone" — that it was a double shame to see her ripping up her books. Ms. Keating would *not* be amused.

Something rustled in the bushes. I looked up just in time to see Kabungo running off with her arms in the air.

"Oh, Kabungo," I said to myself.

"Mi-oo," said Bun.

⊙

I spent the next ten or fifteen minutes sitting on my front step, staring at the page Kabungo had ripped out of her alphabet book. Or at least I tried to look at it. But every time I spread it on my lap, Bun would jump on top of it.

My Aunt Ev always says, if you want a cat to appear, just open a book.

When Bun chased after a squirrel, though, I was able to get a proper look at the scribbles. All I could make out was three faces connected by a long dotted line.

There was a girl's face, a big smiling face and — a cat's.

The girl seemed to be wearing sunglasses. Kabungo has always been very interested in my sunglasses. She calls them sungobbles.

If that picture was supposed to be me ...

"Maybe," I wondered out loud, "it's a map."

If that was true and the girl *was* me, maybe my house was the starting point?

It was worth a try.

I grabbed a garbage bag and tossed the old shoe into it, in case it was important in some way. With cavegirls, you just never know.

◉

The next spot on the map, following the line from my face, was the big smiling face.

I had to think about that one for a long time. It didn't really look like anyone I knew. Except ...

There was one person in town who never stopped smiling, not even for a second.

I made my way to Gobshaw's Drug Shop. When I got there and looked through the

glass at Mr. Gobshaw (of course he was smiling), I wondered. I held up the drawing and compared the two faces.

Though Mr. Gobshaw did smile a lot, he definitely did *not* have a spike of green hair. In fact, he didn't have any. Besides, Kabungo is generally nervous about getting too close to any store. Probably because she's been shooed out of so many of them. So I scrapped that idea.

For the next half hour I paced up and down the street, just thinking, getting more and more frustrated by the minute. I was close to ripping up the map and storming home when I remembered one of my personal rules.

When you're not sure where to turn in life, turn to a bulletin board.

As usual, the Main Street bulletin board was buried in flyers. *Fifty percent off zebras and*

pancakes! said one of them (Mr. Gobshaw's).
Re-elect Mayor Pyecrust! said another.

I'd seen most of them before. But in between all the old posters was a new one.

The pumpkins ... are gone.
The jack-o'-lanterns ... are here.
Come and see.
This Halloween.
Miss VeDore, 318 Main Street.

I took another look at the smiling face on the map.

What if it's not a person, I wondered, but a pumpkin?

I ran down the street. A theory isn't any use unless you test it.

As soon as I got to Miss VeDore's, I knew I was on the right track. Though the gate in

front of her mansion was locked, *something* was sitting just inside it.

It was a smiling jack-o'-lantern — with a big green stem.

And sitting just outside the gate was …

A banana peel.

I tossed the peel into the garbage bag with the old shoe.

"Two down," I said to myself, unfolding the map, "and one to go."

The last face, the cat, could have been the hardest to track down. After all, a cat can mean so many things ("and it usually does," as my aunt would say).

By that point, though, I'd learned to think like a cavegirl. So instead of trying to track down Bun or tramp through the pet shop, I headed straight for Lion's Park. Call it a hunch.

In the middle of the park, not far from Kabungo's family tree, was a rusty soup can. Next to the can was a giant arrow made out of a dozen large stones. The arrow pointed to a bike path that led straight north, out of town.

I shook my head and threw the soup can into the bag. And off I went.

After about twenty minutes of wandering down the bike path, lugging the garbage bag behind me, I found myself walking faster. That's because the path bent right around the Star City Nuisance Grounds (the "Dump" to most people).

I am not a fan of garbage or its smell. I just wanted to skip right past it and get on with finding Kabungo and …

I stopped in my tracks.

Every so often, a person has a Eureka Moment, when suddenly something they have

been struggling to figure out puzzles itself together all at once, like magic.

Well, when the *smell* of garbage coming through my nostrils mixed with the *picture* of Kabungo in my head, there was a powerful reaction.

The old shoe ... the banana peel ... the soup can.

The Nuisance Grounds, I almost shouted.

I took a last deep breath of sort-of-fresh air, plugged my nose ...

And walked through the gate of the Star City Nuisance Grounds.

I had maybe taken two or three steps when I heard a voice say, "Hello, there. Lovely day, isn't it?"

It was the most peaceful-sounding voice I'd ever heard. I looked around to see where it was coming from.

Not far from the gate was a kind of silver trailer. An old man (or his head, at least) was sticking out of the sunroof. It was kind of funny, because the trailer looked like a toaster and the old man — he was on the pale side — looked like a slice of bread that needed to be pushed back down for another minute.

I nodded. I kept walking.

The old man kept talking. "Nothing quite like a sunny autumn day. Clear skies. Fresh air. Perfectly lovely. DON'T GO ANOTH-ER STEP!"

I didn't. Though I did jump a foot in the air.

I looked back at the man, wondering what his problem was. As far as I could tell, he was just an ordinary white-haired old man. He actually had a beard, only it was so pale, you could barely see it.

I didn't recognize him at all, but he was obviously the King of the Garbage Dump.

"Can't just march in, I'm afraid," he said, growing peaceful again and leaning on the top of the trailer. "Not a playground. Though

a playground *is* a lovely place, especially on such a calm, clear-skied day. Nope. Have to have garbage. Something to dump."

As it happened, I did have garbage with me — a whole bagful. I held it up high.

"Ah!" said the man, standing up very straight. "And what do we have today?"

I told him — an old shoe, a banana peel and a soup tin.

"Lovely. Just lovely. You may proceed," he said, waving his hand.

While I stood wondering if I should bow first, the King of the Garbage Dump ducked down into his trailer. So I proceeded.

I was about to toss my bag onto a pile on my right, when —

"HOUSEHOLD GARBAGE TO THE LEFT," cried the old man, popping back out of his toaster.

I shuddered and tossed the bag to the left.

"Lovely, lovely," he said. "Have a *very* lovely day."

I didn't realize it before then, but a garbage dump is actually pretty interesting. It's the only place in the world where you can find a vacuum cleaner and a hula hoop and a dead Christmas tree all tangled into one crazy sculpture.

I was swatting away flies and trying my hardest not to think about rats when I heard a rustling sound coming from a giant pile of boards and sticks.

Something was crawling out of a hole in the pile ...

I got ready to scream. And then I did. But I didn't scream, "Rat!"

"Kabungo!"

"Belly!" she cried right back, galloping up to me.

So many questions tried to rush out of my mouth at once that they got stuck. Before I could unstick them, my friend ran back to the giant pile. She stretched her arms out wide.

"Prize!" she cried, smiling her biggest cavegirl grin.

I raised my eyebrows. *That* seemed to unstick a few questions. I picked one.

"What?" I said.

"Prize," she said again. "Hopping bird day!"

Technically, my birthday wasn't for another seven months. It's the thought that counts, I guess.

"Umm ... thanks, K," I said, staring at the big pile. "What is it?"

"Bird day house," she said proudly.

And before I could stop her, she crawled back through the hole and vanished.

"Belly, come!" she yelled through the hole.

If she thought I was going to crawl on my hands and knees through garbage and squeeze through a dark hole like a rodent ...

"Hurry, Belly. See!"

She was sounding a little anxious.

"BELLY!" she screamed, poking her head back out of the hole.

If her face had looked angry, we probably would have had another big fight and been right back where we started. But she didn't look angry. She looked disappointed. Her big cavegirl eyes swelled up until they almost took over her face.

"Coming, K," I said, sighing.

I rolled up my sleeves, crouched down ...

and made my way through the hole.

No sooner had I crawled inside than my friend grabbed my hand and yanked me to my feet.

"Which?" she said.

Which can mean a lot of things to Kabungo. Usually, it means "Well?" or "What do you think?"

Before I could decide *which*, though, I had to let my eyes adjust.

Luckily, there were plenty of cracks between the boards to let in light.

It was a long time before I answered my friend. If I wasn't sure what to say it was because I wasn't sure what to think. Sometimes you just have to back away and let your brain make its own decisions.

And mine decided, at last, that it was ... impressed.

In the middle of the room was a long black dining table (slightly scratched) with two mismatched chairs at either end. There were framed paintings on the walls, though they had holes in them (the paintings *and* the walls). There was even a grandfather clock, though it wasn't ticking and didn't have any hands.

All things considered, the "house" was at least twice as nice as Kabungo's cave. It must have taken her forever to build. Her whole treasure hunt, too, showed so much planning and cleverness.

"You did all this for *me?*" I said at last, too flattered to care that I was dirty and exhausted and there were eggshells in my hair.

"Ya ya," she said, giving me her Humongous Cavegirl Hug.

After I apologized to Kabungo — she

wasn't a thief, just a garbage picker — I took another look around the birthday house. The table was set with two chipped plates and two toothbrushes. A pair of sungobbles (with one lens missing) hung from a nail in the wall. There was even a (cracked) vase full of dandelions on a stand in the corner.

But in its own way, the house was beautiful.

"Bird day cake?" said my friend, holding up a dead seagull.

"Oh, Kabungo," I sighed.

◉

As we made our way out of the dump, I tripped and landed on a pile of — I think it was rotten cabbages. Kabungo scooped me up and even helped pick some of the bugs off my clothes (though she did eat a few of them).

I looked back to see what I'd tripped on.

It was a xylophone.

I picked it up. Because it gave me an idea.

"Enjoy your day, girls," said the king, rising out of his toaster. "Really nothing like a sunny afternoon. Clear skies. Fresh air. SURRENDER THE XYLOPHONE!"

I jumped.

"Rule number one," he went on a lot more calmly, pointing to a sign I hadn't noticed before.

The sign said NO SCAVENGING.

"I'm ... sorry," I said.

"*Have* Belly," said Kabungo, grabbing the xylophone from me. Then she marched right out of the gate with it.

The King of the Garbage Dump didn't say a word to her. He must have known what I was thinking because he said, "Oh, that's dif-

ferent. Kabungo's family."

My jaw dropped.

"Bye, Grandpa!" yelled Kabungo.

"Him, too?" I gasped, catching up to her, wondering how many surprise grandpas one cavegirl could possible have.

My friend grabbed her stomach and made a noise. It was laughter, I think.

"Belly, joking!" she said. She grabbed her stomach again (it was either laughter or indigestion) and waved at the King of the Garbage Dump.

He waved back — then popped back down into his trailer.

◉

"X fir ..."

Back at the cave, Kabungo and I were sitting by the fire. *Amazing A to Z* (with the ele-

phant page taped back in place) was open on the floor.

"Come on," I said. "You *know* it." I tapped on the real xylophone. "X is for ..."

"X fir ... fir zoo-loo-fun, Belly?"

Close enough.

"Yes!" I said. "You've got it, K!"

She grinned. I really had to get her a new toothbrush.

After that, Y for Yo-yo and Z for Zebra were a cinch, even if Kabungo did try to bite the zebra.

I closed the book. I couldn't believe it. My friend had done it. She knew her alphabet. I finally taught her.

It's not too often that I achieve one of my major life goals. But really, I was a lot prouder of Kabungo.

I'm always telling people, "Kabungo's a lot

smarter than you realize." Some day, I think everyone in Star City will understand it — and appreciate her, like I do. Some day soon.

"Done!" cried my friend, tossing *Amazing A to Z* into the fire.

Well, maybe not *too* soon.

EIGHT
Trigger Cheats!

I LOVE HALLOWEEN. It's not just the candy (though it *is* the candy). It's the everything. The jack-o'-lanterns, the ghastliness, the magic way it changes an everyday place like Star City into something extra-special.

But with Halloween only a day away, there was still lots of work to do. A big pumpkin was sitting outside the cave, waiting to be carved. And I still didn't have a costume.

Neither did Kabungo, for that matter.

I tackled the pumpkin first. I did the cutting

and Kabungo carried away the guts. When we were finished, I lit a candle and sat it inside our brand-new jack-o'-lantern. Kabungo was so impressed that she dragged Bun outside, too. He took one quick look at the jack-o'-lantern, said, "Marr," and trotted back inside.

"If you want to impress a cat, climb Everest first. It's good practice." My Aunt Ev told me that once.

"Have you thought of a costume yet?" I asked Kabungo.

She tilted her head.

"You know — what you want to be for Halloween?"

She bit her finger.

"Kay, know," she said finally.

"What?"

"Cavegirl," she said, skipping back inside.

I would have sighed, but I didn't have time. I decided I'd pop into Gobshaw's to see if any of their costumes interested me.

I was halfway across Main Street when I tripped on my shoelace — and fell flat on my face.

"Haw! Haw! Haw!"

I looked up. I didn't see anyone.

I looked a little higher. Sitting on a lamp-post was a gigantic black bird. A raven.

It flew off.

I stood up. I brushed myself off. I should have been embarrassed. But no, I was *inspired* ...

As soon as I got home, I took an old hooded sweatsuit and glued about a thousand black feathers onto it (they were on sale at Gobshaw's). Then I painted a pointy birthday hat yellow, poked a couple of holes in

it and — presto — my raven costume was complete.

The year before, I'd dressed up as a doctor. The year before that, a dentist. But the *raven* was my least boring costume in years. Besides, ravens are just about the smartest and most interesting birds on the planet, according to Mr. Grisby, my science teacher.

And they *scream* Halloween.

◉

It was exactly six o'clock on October 31st when I showed up in costume at the cave, with a pair of treat pails. I wanted to get an early start. The best candy goes fast. Besides, I had a nine o'clock curfew.

I relit the jack-o'-lantern (it grinned), then banged on the side of the cave with a rock. A pair of eyes sparkled in the dark …

then vanished. In a few seconds, they reappeared.

"TURKEY BIRD!" cried Kabungo,
charging out, bow drawn.

For the next few minutes, I ran up and
down the street, dodging arrows.

When my friend stopped to gather them
up (she only has six), I flung back my hood,
lifted up my beak and screamed, "It's ME!
Beverly!"

Kabungo raised *her* eyebrows, for once.

"Belly, why?" she said.

And so I patiently re-explained, for the
millionth and hopefully last time, all about
Halloween and costumes and trick-or-treating.

My friend scratched her chin and raced
back into the cave.

A minute later, she came back out, wearing

her beast furs, her face paint and her snake-skin pouch.

I'm not sure whose grin was wider, Kabungo's or the jack-o'-lantern's.

"Trigger cheats!" she said.

◉

Most trick-or-treaters go to as many houses as they can as fast as they can and hope for the best.

I prefer a more organized approach: a hit list. The houses on my hit list are where you're guaranteed to get either above-average candy or some kind of surprise that makes them unmissable.

My hit list hasn't changed in quite a few years.

Gobshaw's Drug Shop

The Sunset Club
Miss VeDore's

Our first stop — we had to get there before his shop closed at six-thirty — was Mr. Gobshaw's. He was famous for his Halloween surprises.

On the way, we passed three kids wearing white sheets.

"Spoooks," said Kabungo, shaking a little.

I glared at her in a way that I hoped said, "Remember? It's pretend."

"Ohhh member Belly," she said, reading my mind (and grabbing my arm).

Usually the Gobshaws decorate the outside of their shop for Halloween, but this time there was nothing. Not even a spider. I was a bit disappointed.

"Are you coming in, Kabungo?" I asked.

"Nnn," she said, shaking her head. There were a few too many "spoooks" filing in and out of the place for her. So she waited outside while I investigated.

The second I opened the door, there was a scream — an electronic one. I guess it was Mr. Gobshaw's new doorbell.

Now this is more like it, I thought.

Inside the shop, every last wall and shelf — even the ceiling — was covered in all things Halloweeny. Cobwebs, bats, cats. There was even a rat or two. And, yes, a million spiders.

It was *perfect*.

"Hi!" said a smiling vampire who looked a lot like Mr. Gobshaw.

"Hello!" said a smiling witch who looked a lot like Mrs. Gobshaw. She was stirring a cauldron.

"So," said the vampire. "Which will it be?"

"Which?" I said, puzzled.

"That's *me*," said Mrs. Gobshaw, cackling.

I wasn't sure if she was being funny or not.

Mr. Gobshaw went on, "I mean, which will it be? Trick ..."

"Or treat," finished his wife, sprinkling something into the cauldron.

I was about to say "treat" when Mr. Gobshaw said, "Tricks are 50 percent off."

"And treats are 75 percent off," said Mrs. Gobshaw.

"Off what?" I said.

"Free," said Mr. Gobshaw, picking at his fangs. "Off free."

I smiled. My treat — I'm not sure what would have happened if I'd picked "trick" — was a jumbo sugar-coated marshmallow skeleton on a stick. Those would normally cost $3.99 in their shop.

I was impressed. Mr. Gobshaw dropped it into my pail.

"Don't get into too much mischief!" cried Mrs. Gobshaw as I left.

"Get into just the right amount!" cried Mr. Gobshaw.

I laughed. With Kabungo, that wouldn't be a problem.

◉

Next on our hit list was the Sunset Club — and not only because they gave out more candy than anyone in town. I also wanted to say hi to my Uncle George.

The Sunset Club was on the far side of town, so I thought we might as well stop at a few houses along the way.

They were barely worth the effort. The first lady gave out raisins (her lawn was cov-

ered with 'em). The second gave out gum-balls — exactly one gumball per kid. Kabun-go spat hers halfway across the street.

"Eck. *Not* tasty," she said, wiping her tongue on a lamppost.

My friend hit the jackpot, though, when one man who had given out all his candy started passing out beef jerky. Kabungo calls it "shoe meat."

"*That's* candies!" she said, wolfing hers down.

There were so many kids outside the Sunset Club that we had to wait in line. I knew it would be worth it, though.

Because it's an apartment building, all the residents pool their candy in a gigantic tub and just give out handfuls and handfuls till they run out. It's pretty great.

The line was long, but it was moving fast.

"And here *you* are and you and you," said a gentle voice at the front of the line.

I thought it sounded ... familiar.

"And one for you and you and your lovely friend here and ..."

I wondered ...

"Some lovely blue ones for you and pink ones for you and — MORE GUMMY BEARS!"

It was the King of the Garbage Dump. But he was the King of Halloween now. He was wearing a crown and an orange cape. He even had a scepter with a little pumpkin on the end. His throne might have been a lawn chair and his servants the other Sunset Club residents. But it's the idea that counts, as my Uncle George would say.

I wondered where *he* was ...

"MORE LICORICE!" cried the king.

Kabungo and I got to the front of the line just as a few other servants dumped fresh sackfuls of candy into a big treasure chest. The King of Halloween reached into the chest and gave Kabungo and me several handfuls each.

Now our pails were heavy.

"Have you seen my Uncle George?" I asked his majesty.

"Gone," said the king.

"Gone where?"

"To see the queen," he said.

I smiled. Because I knew exactly what he meant.

"Have a *lovely* evening," said the king, waving his scepter as we walked away.

◉

If the garbage dump man was the King of Halloween, you could bet that Miss VeDore

was the queen. Every year, she did something special, something magical and uncanny.

By the time we got to her place, it was dark. The sun sets so fast, sometimes, it's like a coin falling into a piggy bank.

As dark as it was on Main Street, it was darker still in front of Miss VeDore's. The trees around her mansion blocked the moon out completely.

All I could really see was a single grinning jack-o'-lantern sitting inside the iron gate.

I touched the gate ...

It squealed open.

"Spoooking," said Kabungo, grabbing my arm.

I told her it was all right and didn't she remember Miss VeDore, the nice lady she'd had tea and biscuits with once?

Kabungo tasted her finger.

"Ohhh kay," she said at last. But as we passed through the gate, she squeezed my arm tighter than ever.

We moved through the trees and down the winding path, with only the light of one jack-o'-lantern to guide us.

This is where my friend came in handy. Night and day are the same to cavegirl eyes.

When I stepped on a branch, Kabungo arched up like a cat. A good cavegirl is always on guard.

We followed one curve and another. There was a definite *glow* at the far end of the path.

And something else, too.

Voices.

The light grew brighter. The voices louder. I heard a scream. I heard laughter. We rounded the corner ...

And there it was.

It was Halloween.

Spread across Miss VeDore's backyard, as thick as jam, were jack-o'-lanterns. Hundreds of them. On the lawn. In the garden. Floating in the bird baths. Sitting, even, in the trees. Grinning a thousand different grins.

It was ghoulish. It was beautiful. It was everything Halloween should be.

But as many jack-o'-lanterns as there were, there were twice as many people — young and old, dressed up or not, standing around talking, eating pumpkin cookies and drinking punch.

To be honest, I really wasn't sure how Kabungo would react. Crowds really aren't her thing.

As she looked around, her eyes doubled in size.

But she didn't take off.

No ... she *smiled*.

"Pardeeng!" she cried.

I smiled. Kabungo finally "got" Halloween.

She dropped my arm like a dead snake and ran into the crowd. She went straight past a toddler in an elephant costume without even trembling. A minute later, when I caught a glimpse of her chatting with the Gobshaws, I smiled again. It was nice to see her fitting in.

I made my way through the crowd, hoping to track down the cookie table. I bumped into a woman in an enormous dress (it looked like a wedding cake), wearing an enormous wig (it looked like frosting) and holding a pair of opera glasses.

At first I didn't recognize her. And then I did.

It was Ms. Keating, the librarian.

"Oh, don't look so shocked, Beverly," she said, laughing. "After all, one can't be a librarian *all* the time." She looked over her opera glasses at me.

When a librarian looks over her opera glasses at you, you know she's serious.

"Hungry?" she said, handing me one of the cookies from the stack she was holding. It looked like a gingerbread man, only with a pumpkin head.

I tried it. It was delicious. No wonder she'd taken so many.

"There's some punch around here some-where, too," she said, nibbling. "If you're thirsty."

Ms. Keating looked over her opera glasses at me again. I decided I was thirsty after all.

The yard was so crowded and there were so many people wanting to say hello that it

took me forever to find the punch. And when I finally did find it, I also found Kabungo bent over the bowl, licking up the punch like a happy cat.

"Punch you Belly?" she said, looking up, her chin dripping.

"Maybe another time," I said.

"Kay," she said, dipping her whole head in the bowl.

I sighed. And then I gasped. Only this time, it wasn't because of Kabungo …

High above us, on the mansion balcony, a light had appeared. I squinted. It was a jack-o'-lantern. It had the widest, weirdest grin I'd ever seen, the most golden glow. It looked like it was *floating*. It floated from the far end of the balcony to the very edge and sat down on the railing, like it was watching us.

A second light appeared beside it. A tall candle held by a woman in a black dress, with a pointed black hat. A witch.

Miss VeDore.

Pretty soon everyone was watching her, wondering what she was up to. The whole yard went *dead*.

"Halloween," she said, "is coming."

The witch smiled as something hopped up onto the railing and crawled towards her.

"Halloween," she said, "is *here*."

Miss VeDore scratched Halloween under his chin. He looked like he was wearing ... a cat mask.

The witch clapped her hands.

"Trick," she said, "or treat?"

"Treat!" said almost everyone.

The witch shook her head. She waved her hand mysteriously.

"No," she said. "Trick *and* treat. Look out below!"

And she pushed the jack-o'-lantern over the railing!

Everyone jumped aside before it shattered on the ground. Gold flew everywhere.

Gold *coins*. The pumpkin was stuffed with 'em.

Kabungo grabbed one. She squinted at it. She took a bite — and made a lemon face.

As I rushed towards her, she spat out — chocolate.

They were *chocolate* coins.

"Nnn," said my friend, shaking her head. "Not tasty."

"Look!" cried someone, pointing up.

A hundred someones lifted their heads just in time to see ...

A bird. An enormous bird. A raven. The

same raven, I was sure, that had laughed at me the day before.

"Maxim!" cried Ms. Keating, right behind me.

"Maxim?" I said.

"My pet raven," she said. "He escaped last week. Maxim! Come down here at once!"

But Maxim didn't listen. Instead, he perched on the balcony railing, playfully pecking at Halloween. The raccoon slapped him back. They acted like old friends.

Who knows? Maybe they were.

"Brilliant!" said a voice over my shoulder.

It wasn't Ms. Keating. It was my Uncle George! Or at least, it was a zombie who looked a lot like my Uncle George ...

"Brilliant costume," he said, smoothing down my feathers. "Where on earth did you get the idea?"

As I wondered whether or not to tell him about Maxim, a certain bird swooped down — and landed on my head.

"I guess that answers that," said my uncle, laughing.

"Haw! Haw! Haw!" said a certain bird, flying off.

My uncle reached into his pocket.

"Happy Halloween, Beverly," he said, slipping a marshmallow witch (my favorite) into my hand.

"Happy Halloween, Kabungo," he said, slipping a salami into hers.

My friend leaped up. She started hopping around on one foot and swinging the salami around and scratching herself.

"Does she have fleas?" my uncle whispered into my ear.

"It's her victory dance," I whispered back.

"Though I should probably buy her some more flea powder, just in case."

My uncle laughed. His false teeth sparkled in the moonlight.

"Toooofs," said Kabungo, dropping the salami, eyes widening.

Luckily, she was distracted by something. A buzzing. It sounded like ... an airplane.

I looked up.

It *was* an airplane. A tiny old-fashioned plane flying low over Miss VeDore's mansion.

The whole crowd stared up at it.

"Grandpa!" cried Kabungo. Because that's who was flying the plane — the old man from the cabin in the woods. He was still wearing his odd leather hat — a *pilot's* hat.

Strapped into a seat behind him, looking shockingly calm, was his pet mountain lion, Nikolaas.

"Prettige Halloween!" cried the old man at the top of his lungs, waving. *"Prettige Halloween!"*

"That means Happy Halloween in Dutch," said Ms. Keating over my shoulder.

I jumped. I forgot that, wherever a librarian is, she's always right over your shoulder.

"Ha ha funny!" said Kabungo, jumping up and down and waving. *"Prettige Halloween,* Grandpa! *Wat een aangename verrassing voor ons allemaal!"*

My eyebrows just about jumped off my face.

"That's Dutch for 'What a pleasant surprise for all of us!'" said Ms. Keating.

"You speak *Dutch?*" I said to Kabungo.

"Duh Belly," she said, rolling her eyes.

Never underestimate a cavegirl.

Ms. Keating and my uncle waved good-

bye — and walked off together. I've always thought they'd make the perfect couple ...

I was pooped. When I saw Miss VeDore's rocking chair, I decided the jack-o'-lantern sitting on it had rested long enough, and it was my turn.

Even Kabungo looked tired. She lay down on the grass beside me.

"So? What do you think?" I said.

"Tasty," said my friend, picking something out of the grass and popping it into her mouth.

"I mean about *Halloween*. Trick-or-treating. The party?"

Kabungo chewed the something — and then her finger.

"Fun," she said at last.

I laughed.

"Do you know what this means?"

Kabungo didn't answer. She was busy watching a moth fly around her head.

"It means we actually have something in *common*, K. Who knows? Maybe it's not the only thing."

The moth landed on her nose. Before I could stop her, she stuck her tongue out like a frog — and swallowed the moth.

Then again, maybe it *was* the only thing ...

◉

We were halfway back to the cave when Kabungo stopped in her tracks — and took off in the opposite direction.

I hesitated — it was dangerously close to my curfew — but decided to follow her.

"Curiosity killed the cat," as my Aunt Ev would say. "But at least it had an adventure on the way."

Our journey ended in Lion's Park. Kabungo stuck the handle of her treat pail between her teeth and scaled her family tree.

I set my pail down and climbed up after her.

Kabungo was standing in the big V, gazing up at the moonlit branches.

She took a deep breath.

"Mom?" she said. "Dat Belly."

I looked up. I didn't quite see what Kabungo was seeing. But I understood.

"Hi," I said.

"Dad?" my friend went on, pointing at me. "Belly."

I nodded.

"Small Sitter — Belly. Big Brudder — *listen* Brudder, BAD — this Belly."

I said hi to both of them.

"Kay," said my friend, standing up. She

171

grabbed a handful of treats from her pail —
and tossed them into the air.

"Therego Mom."

Another handful.

"Therego Dad."

Small Sitter got *two* handfuls.

As for Big Brudder, Kabungo carefully
picked a single jawbreaker out of her pail and
crammed it into a hole in a nearby branch.

Once the candy had stopped falling, Kabungo sat down. Then she looked up again.

"Belly ... Belly flimsy too. Belly *sitter*.
New same sitter, kay?"

I wasn't a hundred percent sure what a
"same sister" was. But I was proud to be one,
just the same.

The wind rattled the branches.

My friend looked at me.

"Flimsy ... say nice Belly, kay? Sniff Ka-

bungo. Sunup, sungo. Everever, Belly, kay?"

I smiled.

"Everever," I said.

Kabungo gave me a Strapping Cavegirl Squeeze, then bounded down the tree.

"Come Belly!" she said, waving. "Sniff!"

I laughed and followed her.

After all, when your best friend is a cavegirl, every day is going to be an adventure, whether you want it or not.

And that's a guarantee.

Rolli is a writer, illustrator and cartoonist, and he is the author of dozens of poems and stories for children. He is the recipient of the John Kenneth Galbraith Literary Award, and his work appears regularly in *Ladybug*, *Spider* and *Highlights*.

Rolli lives in Regina, Saskatchewan.

rollistuff.com